COMPOST

D1733591

# COMPOST

## A COSMIC VIEW WITH PRACTICAL SUGGESTIONS

TEXT BY CAROLYN GOLDSMITH

ILLUSTRATIONS BY JEANNE BAUMGARTEN

HARPER COLOPHON BOOKS
Harper & Row, Publishers
New York, Evanston,
San Francisco, London

COMPOST: A Cosmic View with Practical Suggestions
Copyright © 1973 by Carolyn Goldsmith and Jeanne Baumgarten.
For information address Harper & Row, Publishers, Inc., 10 East 53rd Street, New York, N.Y. 10022. Published simultaneously in Canada by Fitzhenry & Whiteside Limited, Toronto.
FIRST EDITION; HARPER COLOPHON BOOKS 1973
LIBRARY OF CONGRESS CATALOG CARD NUMBER: 73-5466
STANDARD BOOK NUMBER: 06-090330-9

# COMPOST

*Plants love leavings.*
*Rotting makes a fine comestible*
    *of dead animals and plants*
            *excrement*
            *garbage.*
*Bacteria make most digestible*
    *the leavings of living things.*

## Manure Varies Greatly in Quality

*Manure, well rotted,*
*Mellow mulch.*
*Holds water full of nutrients*
*Adds warmth to soil*
*And loosens it  . . .*
*For more air space.*

*Manure, well rotted,*
*Mellow mulch,*
*Provides nutritious meals for plants*
*Delivered at a proper pace.*

matter is covered with a layer of soil
and is left to decompose. the com
post making process can only be succ-
essful with moisture air and plen
ty of nitrogen. It is important to
turn a compost heap about once
a week to bring soft material
to the center of the pile and to
distribute the organisms at work.
this also keeps the pile from
compacting. Easily rotted material
pile and fungi. Heap
will cook
bact
d
de
compose
com
pose
de
com
po
se

*The center of a compost pile is made of layers*
    *of rotting vegetable matter, manure, and soil,*
*A chemical hot water bottle working in a secret,*
    *center place*
    *to warm tiny organisms*
    *which grow and gobble and multiply*
        *and*
            *COOK.*

*A warm bacterium feeds hugely*
            *and multiplies promiscuously*
            *and thrives on rot and stink.*

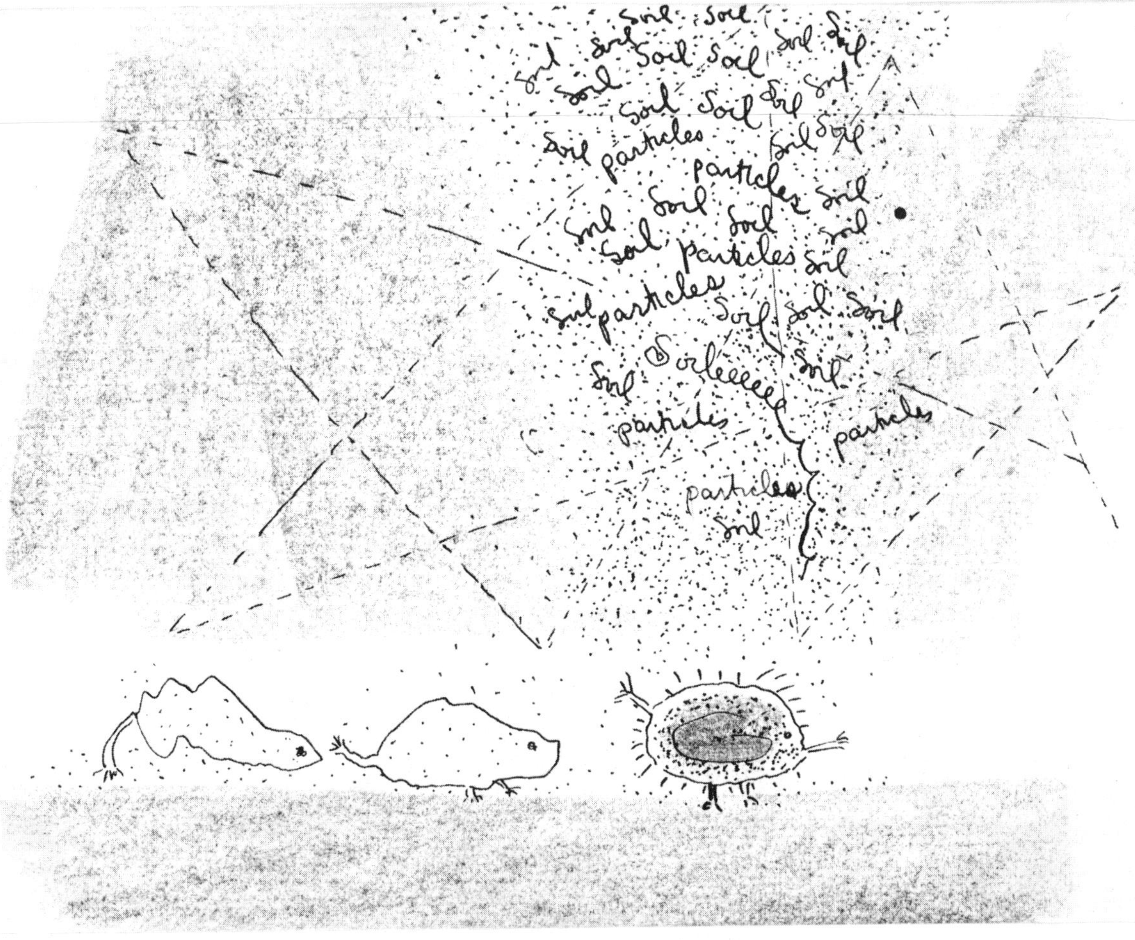

*Outside, the pile is*
*not too hot,*
*not too cold,*
*not too fast,*
*not too slow.*
*Here slower bacteria help*
*humble fungi*
*crumble*
*the warm*
*outer areas*
*of the pile.*

*Breaking down*
*is*
*Building up.*

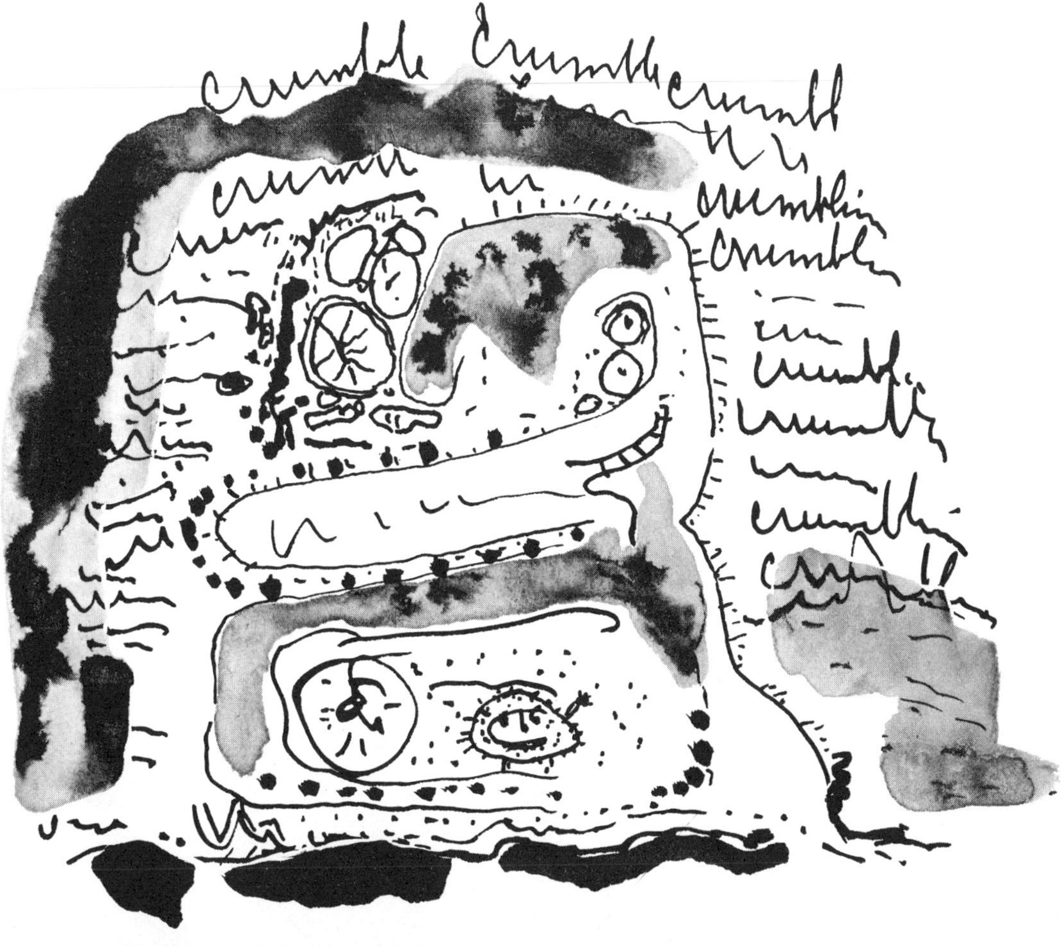
crumble

*Fertile soil is a dynamic living body.*
*It circulates air and water.*
*Water is its blood and air is its breath,*
*carrying life from one part to another.*

*Compost is artifical manure from vegetable matter digested by microoganisms instead of animals.*

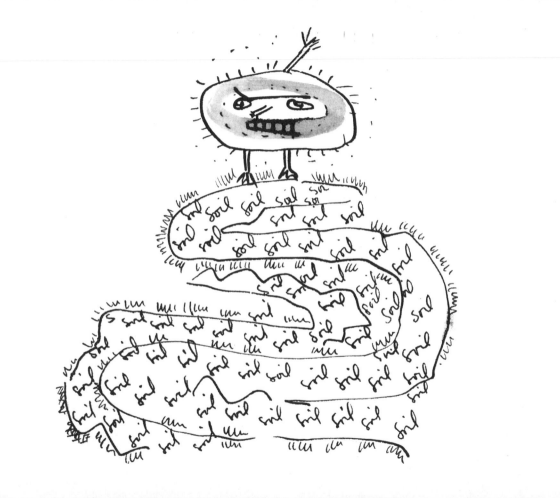

*Giving and taking . . .*
*Humus, well-rotted, enriches clay*
*Clay, unclotted, adds minerals to compost*

*Taking and giving . . .*
*Plants, taking nurture prepared by bacteria*
*Roots, giving gases to promote decay*
*And leaves and stems*
                *dying . . .*
                        *food for microbes and fungi*

completely decomposed
diet of animals most Western.
organic fertil
moisture         soils    need
mature                   nitrogen
compost          manure
compost          or compost    decomposed
must be          must be       rotted
mature,          added, added  inorganic materials
be               added, added  rich in nutrients
different        added, added  dead leaves
rates            added         Leaves
in heap                        leaves .s. .s. .s. .s. .s.
rotted
soft

*HOLES are living space*
  *space for water and air*
*made by creatures large and small*
      *worms and ants*
      *burrowing mammals*
      *digging creatures, like man.*

the burrowing habits of worms make them valuable soil builders......

In the warm, dark earth the worm forms round burrows by pushing its way through soft layers of soil and eating its way through hard layers through which it cannot easily push. At night it pulls vegetable matter into its burrow and during the day it feeds on decaying vegetable matter and soil containing organic material. The burrows make a network of small air passages, making the soil capable of holding air and water. Worms are a great aid in composting. They help break down organic material through their feeding activities. Their nitrogen wastes feed the bacteria active in compost and thus aid the process of decay. If a compost heap is not too high, earthworms will flourish in it. A high heap builds up too much heat in its center parts for worms to survive, but even in such a pile, worms will enjoy the outer portions.

the burrowing habits of worms make them valuable soil builders . . . .

*The worm is devoted to digestion.*
*It moves by eating*
*through large piles of dirt*
*And finds nothing more interesting than pulling soil into*
*and pushing soil out of its intestinal tube.*
*It moves by "passing"*
*Leaving tunnels behind*
*And large piles of casting,*
*Airy, fertile casting.*

clicking sounds while burrowing-click... click... click...

The earthworm is a segmented worm found in warm climates.
Each segment is provided with bristles by which it pulls itself along by contraction... of
no eyes   light senitive   spots   on each   its longitudinal muscles and
segment

*Moving . . . removing*
*Making holes . . .*
*Ants frantically dash*
　　*picking up bits*
　　　　*of this*
　　　　*and that*
　　*carrying trash*
　　　　*from here*
　　　　*to there*

*Seemingly aimless scavengers.*

*But they busily bustle*
*pursuing a task*
*in the ant world*
*unwittingly stirring the Great Mix*
*of time*
*and earth*
*and life.*
*Moving . . . Removing . . .*

*Plants emerge as a natural consequence of
all that is happening
inside the soil body.*

*The slow steady release and joining of bone*
     *and ash with soil and root*
*The hot, fast release of nitrogen from air*
     *and leaf and flesh*
     *greedy gobbling rhythm drawing energy from the*
        *sun*

*Warm and wet promote more energy*
     *excite bacteria and chemicals which*
     *create more heat*
     *make more life.*

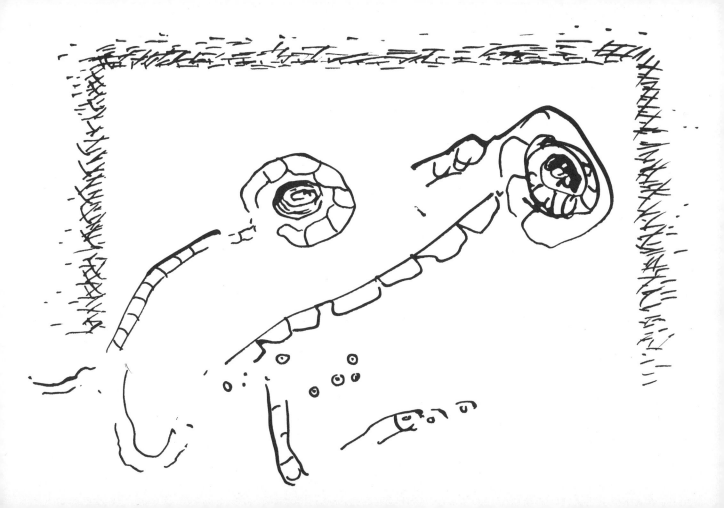

*Warming*
*Wetting*
*Stirring up*

*Small energies*
*Acting on each other*
*Reacting to each other*

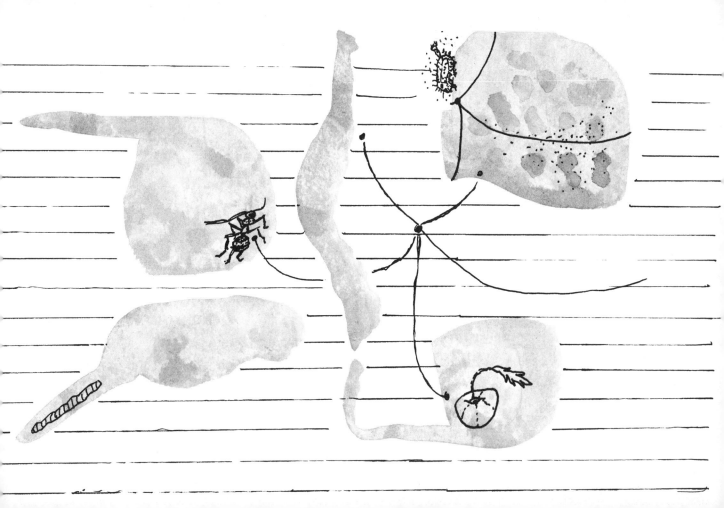

*Death is life.*
*Digesting is transforming,*
*Giving and taking in the continued round,*

*Transforming in a rhythmic dance, circle within circle,*
     *many rhythms intertwined,*
      *micro- and macro- rhythms.*

*The rhythm of life is alternation of movement and rest;*
*a flow of forces, vital forces,*
*alternation of fast and slow*
*faster, slower*
*or in a different way.*
*No standing still*
*No stopping*

*Pauses only*

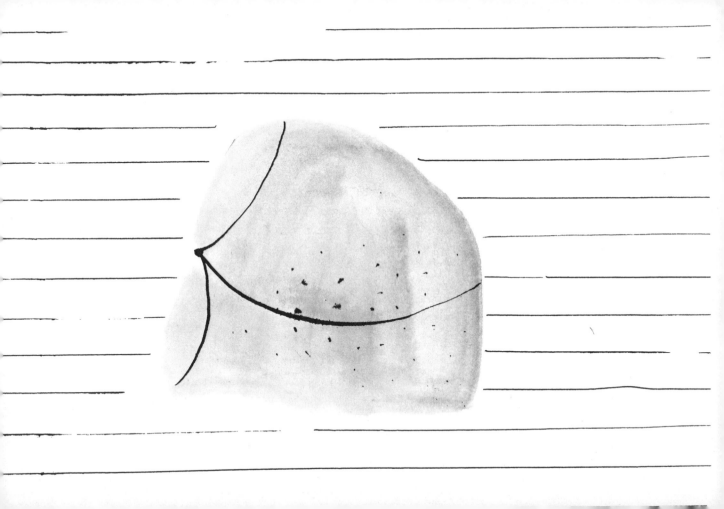

*Pause and swing*
*Cycle within cycle*
*A series of pauses and cycles*
*Huge*
*Complex*
*Choreography . . .*
   *Geologic ages*
   *Floods, earthquakes, and seasons*
   *Dancing a grand ceremonial*
   *and intertwining*
   *the dance*
   *of humbler forces*

*Out of death,*
  *wood ash and bones,*
  *rotting matter,*
  *crumbling stones*
*come vegetation and flesh and bone.*

*A dead bird is crawling with life.*

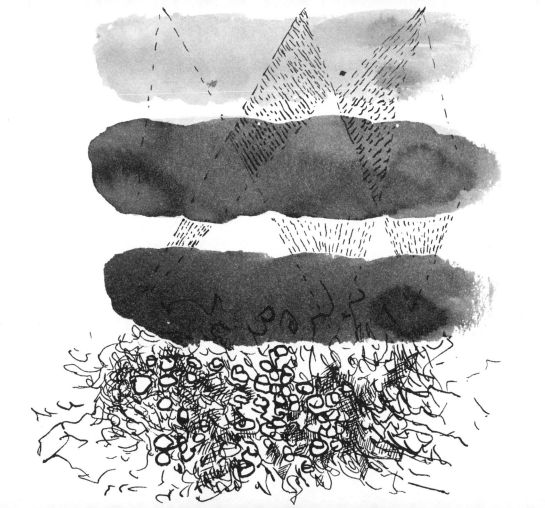

*You*
*Can Stir the Great Mix*

*Recipes for Cooking Compost*

# How to Make a Compost Pile

*Dig a shallow pit or simply loosen the soil in a small sheltered area. The dimensions are optional but an area four-by-four feet or four-by-six feet seems a good size for a small garden. Larger piles are awkward unless you have machinery for turning. Make more piles if you have more materials.*

*Pound two fence posts into loosened soil within the enclosure. Build pile around posts. Start the pile with a layer of branches or other loose vegetable matter to provide circulation of air.*

*Add six inches of green matter (garden clippings, weeds, and so on).*

*Add two inches of manure, a sprinkling of ashes or limestone, and one inch of earth.*

*Moisten.*

*Continue adding layers, introducing garbage in the vegetable layer after the first one.*

*Make the pile up to five feet tall but not higher. It gets too heavy for good aeration and may overheat if it is higher than this.*

*Remove stakes to make ventilation chimneys when pile is five feet high.*

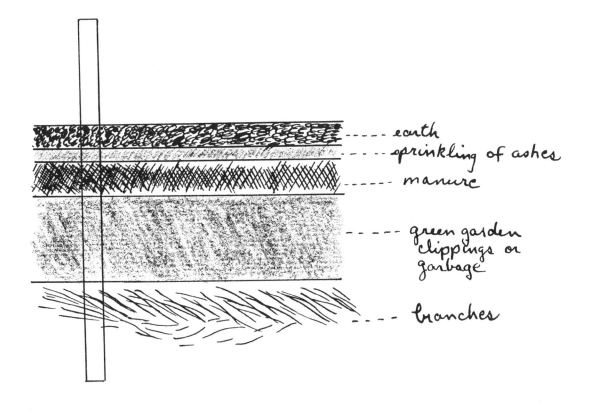

earth

sprinkling of ashes

manure

green garden
clippings or
garbage

branches

## Compost is a Living Thing which needs Warmth, Moisture, and Air TO GROW

*Rain water is the best water. It carries nutrients.*
*Make your pile concave on top to catch the rain.*
*Water during dry weather*
  *but don't soak.*
*Dryness and cold may stop composting altogether.*
*Cover the pile with grass and soil.*
*During extremely cold, dry or wet weather*
*Cover loosely with plastic; or*
*Cover with grass and soil and then plastic*
  *to keep it warm*
  *to keep it moist*
  *to keep it from getting soggy.*
*You don't need to enclose your pile;*
*But an enclosure can help get air to all parts of the pile—*
*improve a compost heap's appearance.*
  *Some people start their piles on top of raised slats or wire*
  *to get air from underneath*
  *as well as from the sides.*

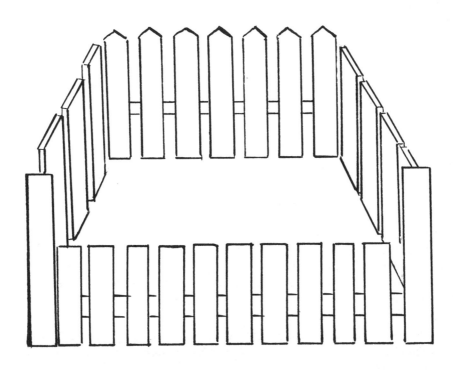

*Turning your compost inside out*
*Redistributes microorganisms*
*And gives them air—*
*Speeds them up.*

Turning

*Turn the pile at the sixth week.*
*Compost should be ripe in ten to twelve weeks.*
*If it is not ripe, turn it again at twelve weeks.*
            *or*
*Turn at third and fifth week—*
*And again at nineth or tenth.*
*Your compost will ripen faster.*
*Enclosures pictured are designed for easy turning.*
*The wire enclosure on the next page (A) is secured by snap fasteners. When the heap is ready to turn, these can be*
*opened and the wire removed from the heap. The enclosure is reassembled nearby and the heap is*
*shoveled into the wire enclosure again.*
*The bin pictured at the far right (B) has two compartments. Compost is shoveled into the empty compartment*
*to turn it. If a second turning is made, the compost is shoveled back into the first compartment. The*
*front of the box is removable for easy use of compost.*
*A second compost may be started in the empty bin after the last turning.*

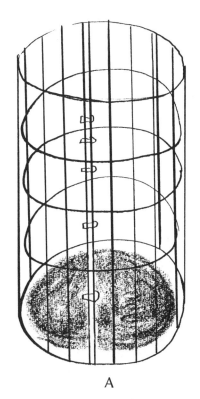

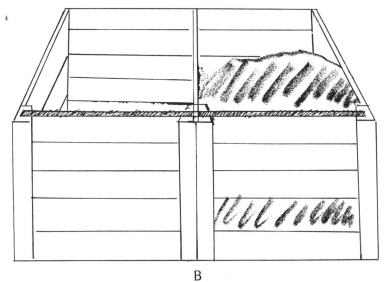

A

B

## Grinding

*Smaller particles make more surfaces*
*for bacteria and fungi to attack.*
*They multiply and work at a furious rate*
*as they get food for energy and body building.*
*Grinding helps any composting, but is essential for . . .*

## Making Compost in 14 Days

*Shred together vegetable matter and manure with a rotary mower or shredder.*
*Mix with rock powders.*
*Make the pile three to five feet high.    Stir.    Moisten.*
*Turn on fourth, seventh, and tenth days. Keep moist.*
        *(University of California recommends turning every two or three days)*
        *Be sure your pile is heating up.*
        *If it isn't add more high nitrogen material (see N, p.78) and turn a day or so later.*
        *If not done in two weeks, turn on fourteenth day. Moisten.*
        *Use on nineteenth day.*

## What is Happening in Your Compost Heap

1.  *A pile five feet tall will heat up to 160 degrees Fahrenheit.*
    *This is a chemical reaction, a result of oxidation. The pile will be reduced to about 3½ feet in four or five days. A metal rod or thermometer can be inserted to see if it is heating. At this point the protective epidermis of the plant matter is broken down by thermophilic (heat loving) bacteria and fungi as well as by the chemical processes.*

2.  *Plants are penetrated by aerobic fungi (fungi which get oxygen from the air).*
    *All the surfaces are covered with a network of thread-like mycelia (body) of the fungi.*

3.  *Aerobic bacteria replace fungi after about three weeks.*
    *These penetrate the cells of the plants by following the fungous threads and by feeding on fungi which die as the temperature lowers. By the end of another three weeks the heating process has nearly ended (six weeks from formation of pile).*

4. *Anaerobic bacteria (those functioning without free oxygen, getting their supply from compounds in the soil) take over as the pile settles.*

*Compost becomes crumbly and finally colloidal (in extremely fine particles in a homogenized state).*

*The pile must not become compacted or water-logged. Compost-building anaerobic bacteria require some air lest putrefaction, or complete degeneration of organic material, take place. Nutrients held in the soil would then be released by chemical and bacterial action in the form of free nitrogen, carbon dioxide, and other gases, salts, and ammonia. Decay must be arrested in time for the building up processes to intervene and produce stable humus. At the tenth or twelfth week, turn the pile to provide air for . . .*

5. *Azotobacter, the aerobic nitrogen fixing bacterium to get to work.*

*This bacterium will not thrive if the soil is acid. Since compost made mainly of vegetable matter tends to be acid, it needs lime or ash added to it to neutralize it. The anaerobic bacterium Clostridium will tolerate more acidity and work side by side with azotobacter in pockets with low oxygen content to fix large quantities of nitrogen in the compost. In three or four months compost should be finished, (about twelve to sixteen weeks from building of pile).*

# No Turning Method — Earthworms

*Pile composting materials in a bin or against a wall in a pile not more than two feet high.*

*Moisten.*

*Allow to ferment for three weeks.*

*When the pile is no longer warm, make some holes and add red earthworms (can be bought or you can find them in old compost heaps or in rotting manure).*

*Add ground garbage, cornmeal, wheat meal, or coffee grounds for worm food.*

*Keep moist.*

*Cover to eliminate light, but do not exclude air.*

*Earthworms will make compost material in about sixty days or less depending on the number of worms and conditions. Worms will multiply very quickly in moist soil with neutral acidity. Use egg shells to keep pile from becoming acid. Worms multiply quickly at temperatures from sixty to seventy—five degrees Fahrenheit; they will become sluggish under sixty degrees and dormant at thirty—two.*

*Use fertilizer, worms and all, and replenish pile with compost material. Be careful not to let pile get higher than two feet (to prevent overheating). Mix well with compost containing worms.*

*Or – expose pile to strong light. Earthworms will go to the bottom of the pile and you can remove top castings and leave earthworms. Feed earthworms. Stir pile. Keep moist.*

## Keeping Earthworms Working through the Winter

*Enclosure A is designed to protect a compost heap through extremely cold winters.*
*A small pile is made inside a chicken wire enclosures.*
*Another fence is built around this enclosure leaving a space of 1½ feet between the two*
*wire pens.*
*In between the two fences leaves, grass, weeds, and other debris is dumped; leaves are*
*piled over the inside heap as well.*
*Earthworms are added when the pile has aged a few weeks, and then the whole structure is*
*covered with a blanket made of burlap bags sewn together.*
*The burlap can be weighted to keep it from blowing.*
*Earthworms may also be raised in pits or boxes during cold winters.*
*Worm boxes may be taken in the basement or other indoor areas which are not too cold.*
*There will be no odor from active earthworm boxes.*
*The enclosure B provides a perfect site for earthworm cultures in a temperate climate.*
*The rock wall protects the pile from wind and holds the winter heat.*
*If such a heap is used for earthworm composting it should be well covered with hay and*
*dirt to conserve moisture.*
*Ventilating holes will help prevent the bottom of the heap from becoming soggy in its*
*deepest parts and in corners. Occasional stirring serves the same purpose.*

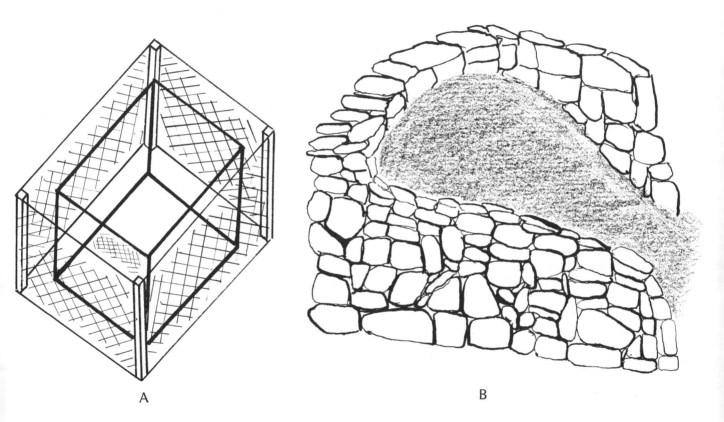

A

B

# Composting at the Planting Site

_Sheet composting_  After the growing season, spread plant material, manure, rock phosphates, ashes, and dig them into the ground or rototill the plot if it is large. Plant in the spring.

_Vertical composting_  Fill shallow trenches between rows of vegetables with compost materials. Next season, before spading used dirt into composted area, dig trenches where vegetables were planted.

_Green manuring_  After the growing season plant area with grass, clover, vetch, or some other legume. Add any kind of organic matter including materials with high C/N ratio (see C/N , p.66) Dig under when cover is green and succulent. If moistened by rain or irrigation, green manures will disintegrate in about six months. They bring valuable nutrients up from subsoils because of nitrogen fixation in legume roots.

_Trench method_  Dig a trench about eighteen inches deep, leaving dirt in a pile beside it. Throw in table scraps, vegetable trimmings, dust from vacuum cleaner, hair clippings, garden trimmings, weeds—any organic matter. Cover each layer with a layer of soil. Moisten each layer well, but do not soak.  Allow to stand one season. Add manure and other animal matter for richer compost and faster decomposing. (We do not use bones and meat scraps because dogs and raccoons dig them up.) Add limestone or sprinkling of ashes and rock powders.

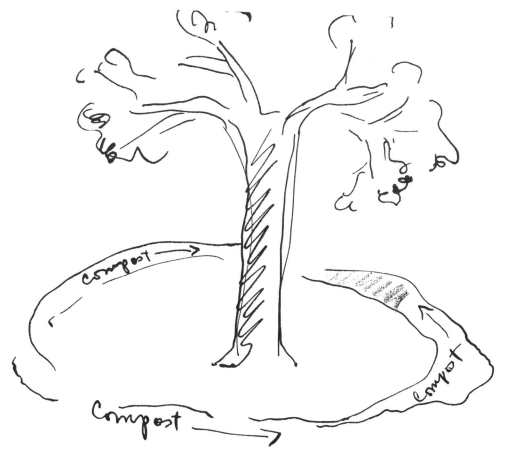

*You can fertilize a tree by composting just outside the drip line. Loosen soil and pile materials up to about three feet.*

# Combining Trench, Bin, and Earthworm Method for a Small Garden

*Make a box four feet long, one to two feet high, and one or two feet wide, with no bottom or top. Dig a trench eighteen inches deep, slightly smaller than the box. Place the box so it rests firmly on the ground and surrounds the trench.*

*Fill the trench with layers of kitchen leavings, manure (sprinkling), green matter, and an occasional small sprinkling of earth.*

*Add earthworms (about 500) after three weeks.*

*During dry season, wet each layer and cover with burlap; put a board over the top of the box.*

*Continue adding layers until the box is filled to the top.*

*Allow to decompose five or six more weeks.*

*Meanwhile start another pit.*

*Empty the box onto a tarp. Allow the tarpful to stand in the sun a few hours. Remove worms which have balled up and gone to the bottom and place them in the other pit.*

*Place the frame on the second pit.*

*Bag the compost for future use, or use immediately as a mulch or fertilizer.*

*Plant in the newly composted area, site of the first pit.*

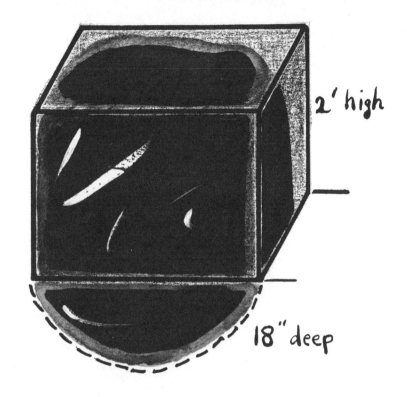

2' high

18" deep

## An Additional No-turning Compost Method: Anaerobic Composting

*Put compost in a large plastic bag.*
*Add plenty of nitrogenous material (manure, bone meal, and the like).*
*Tie securely.*
*Do not open for three months.*

> *or —*

*Make a pile of composting materials on ground that has been turned.*
*Cover pile with black plastic.*
*Pile dirt around edges to seal out air.*
*Leave for about three months.*

*Anaerobic composting has the advantage of saving nitrogen and carbon from being oxydized. Compost made by this method is especially high in these elements. Much less reduction in bulk.*

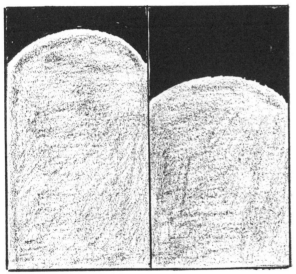

anaerobic                    aerobic

# C/N Ratio

*C/N stands for the carbon :nitrogen ratio in the soil. Microorganisms feed on organic matter containing, among other things, nitrogen and carbon. They use carbon for energy and nitrogen for body building. Under stable conditions microorganisms maintain a C/N in soil of ten; that is, ten parts of carbon to one part available nitrogen.*

*This balance is upset when organic material high in carbon and low in nitrogen (like straw or wood chips) is added to the soil. Excess carbon compounds in the soil stimulate the growth of microbe populations because of extra energy provided by the starch and sugar (carbon compounds) stored in the stems of plants. The microorganisms must have nitrogen to take care of building body proteins. Because they cannot get nitrogen from the plant matter, they borrow it from the soil supply and are thus in competition with plants for the nitrogen supply.*

*This depletion is temporary but may cause plant damage before the process is reversed. The wildly multiplying organisms finally use up the carbon supply and start to die off. Their bodies decay and return the nitrogen to the soil. The soil is then back to normal.*

*To prevent plant injury, materials such as wood chips should be added to the soil in autumn and allowed to stand till spring. If high carbon material is used in an area where plants are growing, high nitrogen material should be added to prevent plant damage.*

# Materials for Compost

*Any organic material that contains at least 1.5 percent nitrogen can take care of its own decomposition without reducing the total nitrogen supply of the soil. This includes organic materials with a C/N ratio of 30:1 or less. Twenty-five or thirty to one is the ideal ratio for composting. Finished compost ready to use for fertilizer or planting has a C/N of 14 to 20:1. It is important that compost not be completely stabilized (10:1) when used as fertilizer because it must function as a stimulus to bacterial growth in the soil.*

## Waste Materials Suitable for Composting

Old, slow working materials, low in nitrogen first (C/N ratios):

Saw dust  150- 500:1
Straw, cornstalks  50-150:1
Peat moss  50:1
Leaves from oak, birch maple  40-60:1
Alder, ash leaves  20-30:1
Manure with bedding materials  20-25:1
Green grass clippings  20-30:1
Vegetable trimmings  20-30:1
Hay from legumes  15:1
Animal droppings  15:1

High nitrogen wastes to speed composting of high carbon materials (figures given in percent):

Blood meal  10-14 N
Feathers, hair  15-17
Horn and hoof meal  10-6
Leather wastes  5-12
Conttonseed meal  7
Fish meal  7
Bone meal  3-4
Peanut shells  3-6
Coffee, tea grounds  2-4
Grasses 1-3 (Legumes—clover,
pea, soy—highest)

It is not important to know the C/N ratio of the materials you wish to compost.

It is important to use a mixture of materials:

 Young and old plant materials (see Materials for Compost p.67)

 High nitrogen material

 A small amount of phosphorous and

  potassium containing material (see Phosphorous p.79 and Potassium p.80)

 Manure, soil, or old compost—for bacteria

 A little lime, unless you want acid compost (see pH, p.87)

Sawdust compacts, so sprinkle it in layers.

Leaves also tend to compact. Stir them with soil or chop them. Spread on the lawn and run a rotary lawn mower over them. Rake up.

Smaller particles (to a point) compost faster than large ones.

Kitchen leavings are high in protein (nitrogen). Fats do not decompose readily, but a small amount (such as in leftover salad) will not retard compost.

Soapy water is not good for most plants (beets don't mind it however!).

Paper ash is not good for compost because it contains acids used in paper-making inimical to plants.

Poultry manure contains more nitrogen than any other manure. It is also high in phosphorous and has some potash. It is well to mix it with litter or compost if applying directly to plants.

*Wash sea weed to remove salt before using in compost heap.*

*Large bones will not disintegrate easily. Grind or break into pieces.*

*Do  not use charcoal. It will not disintegrate.*

*Eucalyptus, camphor, walnut, and laurel leaves should be exposed to weathering for a time before using in compost. Their aromatic oils and alkaloids interfere with decompostion . Grinding these leaves makes them more susceptible to decay.*

*Bacterial activators do little to speed compost according to studies made at University of California and Michigan State University.*

*Do not use coal ashes. They contain sulfur trioxide which produces sulphuric acid when it comes in contact with water. Soft coals also contain too much iron.*

*Citrus peels and other fruit waste are rich in potash.*

*Coffee molds when used alone. Mix with other materials.*

*If manure is not available, earthworms will help compost by adding animal excretions.*

*Feathers are exceptionally high in nitrogen and decay in a season if kept moist.*

# WHEN IS COMPOST "DONE"?

| | Ideal Compost | Faulty Compost | Cause of Failure |
|---|---|---|---|
| Texture | Medium loose. Crumbly. | Dry, powdery. Compacted, soggy. | Overheating, too dry. Lack of air, too wet. |
| Composition | 25-50 percent organic matter; some original material recognizable. | Heavy, earthlike. | Too much dead earth (from ditches, ponds, roads). Such earth should freeze and thaw and be exposed to air for several seasons. |
| Moisture | Like squeezed-out sponge. | Soggy. | See above explanation. |
| Color | Black-brown. | Grey or yellow. Pure black | Too much dead earth. Wrong ferment. See below. |
| Odor | Earthlike. | Putrid. Ammonia smell. | Wrong ferment caused by lack of air, too much water, not enough high nitrogen material. Release of ammonia gas may also be caused by alkaline condition. |
| | | Musty. | Too hot or cold composting causes bacteria to die, molds to grow. |
| pH | Slightly acid or neutral: pH 6 to 7.4 (see pH, p.87). | Acid. | Too wet, not enough air, not enough nitrogen material. |
| | | Alkaline. | Not enough organic matter, 1/3-2/3 original matter should be organic. Too much lime. |

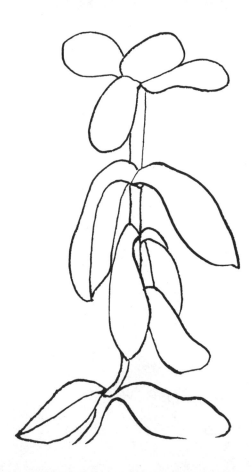

*Plant processes*
        *How it all works*
*Basic principles of plant growth*
*And the relationship of plants to the soil.*

### Respiration

*Respiration is the process of burning or oxidizing foods, mainly carbohydrates, stored by the process of photosynthesis. The energy thus released is used for maintaining the tissues and functions of plants and for building tissues in the growing process. Carbon dioxide and some heat are given off.*

*Phosphates are incorporated as part of the sugar molecule in a so-called energy-rich bond. When oxygen is added this bond is broken by separate action of a series of plant enzymes and energy is released for the building of protoplasm, for the "pumping" action of the roots, and for other life processes.*

## Photosynthesis

*Green parts of plants, when exposed to light, proper temper-
ature, and ample water supply, use carbon dioxide from
the atmosphere and water from the soil to produce carbohydrates and gaseous oxygen.*

*The chloroplasts, microsopic bodies containing green pig-
ment, capture the radiant energy of the sun and transform
it into stored plant energy in the form of starch and sugar.
Some of these carbohydrates are transferred to roots and
fruits from their original storage place in leaves and other
green parts of the plants.*

## Nutrients

There are 16 essential nutrients needed for plants, even though some are used in miniscule quantities. If one nutrient is deficient the balance of the plant metabolism is upset.

| Major nutrients (needed in large quantities). | Nitrogen | Phosphorous | Potassium |
|---|---|---|---|
| | Essential part of plant (and animal) protein. Necessary for growth of leaves and stems. | Necessary for respiration process. Active ingredient in plant cells. Necessary for production of sugar and release and transfer of energy. Promotes flowering, fruiting, and root development. | Necessary for development of chlorophyll (green pigment of plants). Does not enter into molecular structure of tissue. Strengthens plant tissue. Promotes disease resistance. |
| Minor nutrients (needed in smaller supply). | Calcium | | Magnesium |
| | Present in plants mainly in leaves. Helps build plant protein. Aids healthy cell structure. Neutralizes acids in plants. Also helps roots. | | An important component of chlorophyll. |
| | Sulphur | | Iron |
| | Helps provide protein. | | Major element in chlorophyll development and carbohydrate production. |
| Trace elements: | Cobalt, molybdenum, copper, manganese zinc, and others. | | |

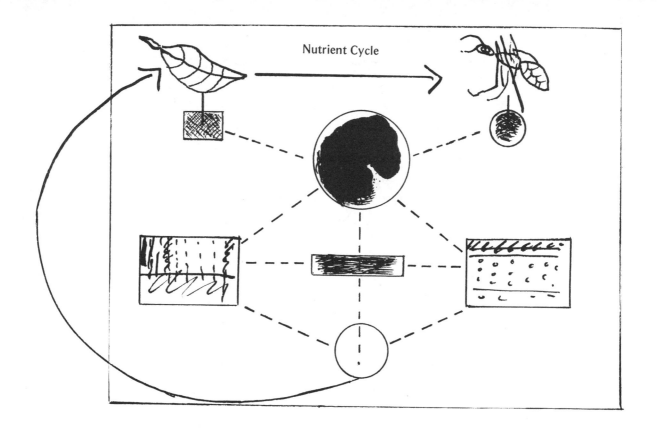

Nutrient Cycle

# Nutrient Cycle

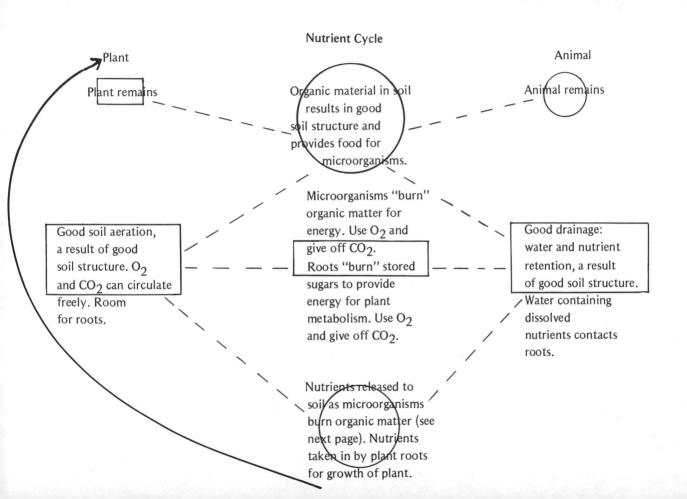

Plant

Plant remains

Organic material in soil results in good soil structure and provides food for microorganisms.

Animal

Animal remains

Microorganisms "burn" organic matter for energy. Use $O_2$ and give off $CO_2$.

Good soil aeration, a result of good soil structure. $O_2$ and $CO_2$ can circulate freely. Room for roots.

Roots "burn" stored sugars to provide energy for plant metabolism. Use $O_2$ and give off $CO_2$.

Good drainage: water and nutrient retention, a result of good soil structure.

Water containing dissolved nutrients contacts roots.

Nutrients released to soil as microorganisms burn organic matter (see next page). Nutrients taken in by plant roots for growth of plant.

*Nitrogen (N) released to soil*

*How It Works*     *Bacteria convert gaseous nitrogen from the air to chemical nitrates and "fix" them in the soil. Some*
*in the Soil*          *nitrogen-fixing bacteria live on nodules on the roots of legumes (pea family). Other  nitrogen is*
                          *released from organic matter as decay organisms break it down.*

   *One group of organisms breaks down raw organic matter to amino acids and ammonia.*

   *A second group changes ammonia to nitrites.*

   *A third group changes nitrites to nitrates, which are soluble and usable by plants.*

   *Other groups fix nitrogen in the soil.*

*Supply*               *Nitrates are very soluble and easily leached from soil beyond the range of plant roots.*
                          *A large supply is needed. Best sources are organic because release of nitrogen is gradual and*
                          *measured by the work of interdependent organisms.*
                          *Overdose of nitrogen results in spindly overgrown plants, delayed fruiting, and susceptibility*
                          *to disease. There is no danger of overdosing with well aged compost or manure.*
                          *Best sources of organic nitrogen are blood meal, fish meal or scraps, cotton seed meal, manure,*
                          *sewage sludge.*

*Phosphorous (P) released to soil*

*How It Works
in the Soil*

*There is a great deal of phosphorous in the soil in the form of mineral or organic compounds. Weathering and breaking down of organic compounds by microorganisms release phosphate ions in the soil. But much of this element becomes 'fixed' in the soil and is not available to plants because it combines so easily with other elements such as iron and aluminum. The latter elements are precipitated especially in acid soil (see pH, p.87). A pH of 6.0 to 7.0 is most favorable for availability of phosphorous to plants. If the soil is alkaline the phosphorous combines with calcium and is unavailable to plants. The root tips of plants take up phosphorous solutions directly from the soil by contact with soil water. Microorganisms use phosphorous freely, so it becomes part of the organic matter in the soil if a generous supply of mineral phosphorous is available.*

*Supply*

*Soils heavily used should have an ample supply of phosphorous even if there are many microorganisms present.
Use of superphosphate, a commercial fertilizer, tends to reduce bacterial population of the soil. Manure in combination with phosphate rock or bone meal effects a slow steady release of phosphates to the soil. Apply one pound to ten square feet every three to five years. It is not easily washed from soil . Best sources are bone meal, phosphate rock, basic slag, activated slag.*

*Potassium (K) released to soil*

*How It Works
in the Soil*

*There are large amounts of potassium in the soil minerals but only 1 percent is available to plants. This 1 percent is locked in the soil in "exchangeable" form as "exchangeable potassium." In this form plants can take in the mineral through direct contact with the roots without its actually becoming part of the soil solution. The free potassium is also available to plants in soluble form but is easily washed away. The exchangeable potassium is insoluble in water and therefore provides an invaluable reservoir of potassium to be drawn on as the plant needs it. Manure and compost can supply plants with potassium in both exchangeable and soluble form.*

*Supply*

*Potassium chloride is a mineral deposit found in desert areas and is often used as commercial fertilizer. This compound has been found to leave a residue of chlorine in the soil which makes an imbalanced soil injurious to plants.*
*Granite dust, greensand (an undersea deposit rich in trace minerals as well), and potassium rock powder are good mineral sources.*
*Wood ash (especially hardwood) and seaweed are especially high in potash.*

## Soil

*This is the kind of
soil you want for good
gardening.*

Fertile Topsoil
or Loam

*Twenty-five percent pore space
filled with water
Twenty-five percent pore space
filled with air
Forty-five percent mineral matter
Five percent organic matter*

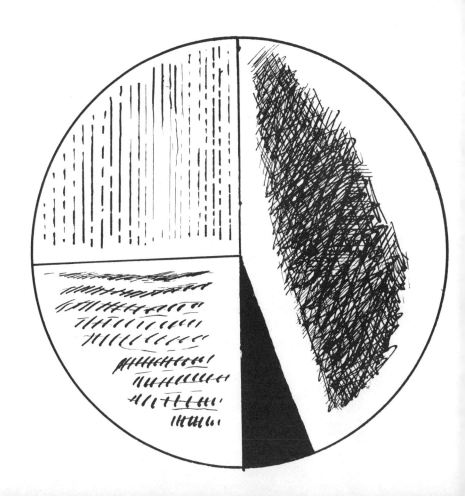

Loam

*Without a small amount of animal and vegetable matter (5-15 percent), soil is as sterile as road dust or pottery clay.*

*Organic matter is the life-giving substance which*

*activates minerals*

*releases nutrients to plants*

*makes the soil porous*

*holds the soil structure so it will sustain life.*

*Organic matter is a reservoir of nutrients which it*

*releases as decaying proceeds.*

*At the same time it becomes food for bacteria.*

*Humus is decayed organic matter which has reached a fairly stable state but is still active.*

*Eventually humus breaks down and loses its structure.*

*Then soil can be swept away by wind and water.*

*Soil must have a constant supply of organic matter to maintain its structure and fertility.*

### What Kind of Soil Do You Have?

*Feel it.*
*Clay is slimy and sticks together.*
*It's hard when dry.*
*It cracks.*
*Silt is smooth like talcum.*
*It molds like clay but not as well.*
*Sand is gritty.*
*Loam is grainy and*
  *Falls apart*
  *When you squeeze it.*

You are feeling the topsoil, the principle feeding area of plants; roots get much nutrition from subsoil as well.

These roots, living and dead, hold good topsoil together.

Suprisingly, the composition of the topsoil has more to do with weather, topography, and plant growth than with the parent rock under the regolith (top decomposed layers).

# Improving Your Soil Texture—Nutrient Holding

| Type of Soil | Composition | Characteristics | Correctives |
|---|---|---|---|
| Loam | Ideal: mixture of sand, clay, and humus. May be sandy, rocky, clayey, silty. | Holds air and water in equal proportions. | This is soil you are aiming for. |
| Clay | Microscopic flat mineral particles. High nutrient value. | Poor water and air circulation. Puddles. Cracks when dry. | Add lime. It flocculates clay (makes fine particles gather in larger units). |
| Silt | Halfway between clay and sand in particle size. Many irregular shaped quartz particles. Low nutrient value. | Puddles. Clods when dry. Not as sticky as clay. | Add with humus, wood products (see C/N ratio, p. 66) partially decomposed compost, rice hulls. |
| Sand | Large irregular particles. Loose structure. Inert (chemically inactive). Made of particles of quartz. No nutrient value | Very good air circulation but no retention of water. Nutrients leach away. Tends to be acid | Add finely-textured humus or compost, peat moss, manure. |

Test your pH. Any type of soil can be too acid or alkaline.

# Hardpan

Hardpan, a hardened layer six inches to two feet below the surface of the earth, can be a local or regional problem.

Locally it can occur from plowing to the same depth year after year, from poor soil structure plus the use of chemical fertilizers, or from compaction by heavy machinery.

Regionally it is caused by topography and weather.

Podzol soils of more or less depth (depending on weather and growth) are underlayed with a layer of clay (claypan) or sometimes with a layer of soil cemented by organic matter.

Desert soils often have a deposit of salts under them, or sometimes on top of them where the topsoil has been eroded (caliche).

In any case, plants are cut off from the nutrients and water in the subsoil and the subsoil cannot be replenished with minerals from above.

Roots cannot penetrate this soil, so plants may drown because of puddling or die from lack of water during the dry season.

Remedy:    Break hardpan with deep plowing or make holes with posthole digger.

Remove as much of hardpan as possible.

Add sand, sifted ashes, and much humus and work them in thoroughly.

Plant cover crop if possible (see Green manuring, p.60).

If hardpan is extensive it may by necessary to install tile drains for removal of water.

# pH: Acidity—Alkalinity of Soil

pH is a chemical term meaning the hydrogen ion concentration. The pH scale runs from 0 to 14, 7.0 being the neutral point. Any soil with a pH measuring less than 7.0 is on the acid side of the scale. A soil with a pH of more than 7.0 is alkaline. Most field crops thrive on a pH of from 6.5 to 7.0. Some plants such as   azalea, raspberry, and oak like a slightly acid soil. Others such as clematis, cabbage, and peas like a slightly alkaline soil (7.0 to 8.0).

The old time gardener tasted his soil to see if it was "bitter" (alkaline), "sour" (acid), or "sweet" (neutral). Soil kits for home use or tests by agricultural experts can give you a more accurate picture. A rough test can be done with litmus paper, which can be purchased at the drug store. If paper turns blue, the soil is alkaline; pink, acid; no change, neutral.

The acidity of the soil is determined partly by the parent rock from which the soil was made and partly by climatic conditions. Arid areas tend to have alkaline soil because there is not enough rain to leach away soil salts. Wet climates tend to have acid soils, especially if the drainage is poor. When decay is slow or there is a constant supply of new vegetable matter under damp conditions, tannic and other acids accumulate in the newly decaying matter. Boggy soils become so acid that they are sterile.

## Correcting High or Low pH

*A pH below 4 or over 9 poisons most plants. At a pH of 4, plants will starve because bacterial life releasing soil nutrients cannot survive. Also, aluminum and manganese in lethal quantities are dissolved by the acids and are fatal to plant life. Salts in strongly alkaline soil dissolve and disperse the humus's structure and make the soil hard and impermeable to water.*

*Crushed limestone mixed with compost can be added to acid soil to neutralize it. Caustic chemical lime should not be used. It can burn plants and destroy organic life in the soil. Lime also has the virtue of adding calcium to the soil (most soils have enough of this element). Lime also conditions heavy soils (see clay, p.85). It speeds bacterial action on green manures when added to compost.*

| *Sources of lime:* | *Effect beside altering pH:* |
|---|---|
| *Crushed limestone* | *Flocculates clay* |
| *Bone meal* | *20 percent phosphorous, 1.5 percent nitrogen* |
| *Dolomite* | *40 percent magnesium* |
| *Marl (lime-clay deposit from stream beds)* | *Works very slowly* |
| *Oyster shells* | *10 percent phosphorous* |
| *Wood ash* | *Some phosphorous and magnesium* |
| *Egg shells* | *1 percent nitrogen* |

*Leaf mold and manure can safely be used in large quantities to correct alkaline soil. Gypsum (calcium sulphate) makes alkaline soil more acid and also conditions the soil. Use with caution.*

# When to Use Compost

*Early spring*  Dig soil to aerate; add organic material and one-half to three inches partially finished compost a month in advance of planting. Top spadeful should be in prime condition.

*Spring*  For planting seeds or potting, screen compost to cull out unfinished parts. Mix with topsoil, half and half. For fertilizing place compost in furrows. Dig in beyond drip line for trees (see Composting at the Planting Site, p.60) Mulch seedlings with partially finished compost and grass clippings to prevent weeds from growing and provide slow fertilizer. Warning: Mulch encourages snails.

*Summer*  Mulch to prevent drying. Keep compost pile wet to prevent over-heating. Cover if storing finished compost.

*Autumn*  Mulch lawns. In cold climates dig in unfinished compost and dead vegetable matter leaves, and the like). Cover compost to save till spring.

*Winter*  Weathering of rain and snow improves soil structure. Avoid digging when soil is wet: it tends to form compacted clods. Dig only when soil falls apart when squeezed. In temperate zones composting of soil can be done in winter.

If soil needs conditioning, compost a season ahead of planting.

For quick feeding or fertilizing pots, make compost water by soaking finished compost and pouring off water.

# Why Use Compost as Fertilizer? Why Use Organic Nitrogen in the Compost Heap?

*Chemical fertilizers such as ammonium sulphate, ammonium nitrate, and sodium nitrate add nitrogen to soil. Why not use them since they are quick acting and effective in increasing the yields of crops? We are finding good ecological reasons for not using inorganic substances in soil and compost:*

*First, we are finding our water polluted by runoff from large-scale agricultural fertilizing and spraying.*

*Second, the structure of the soil is being damaged by not returning organic matter to the soil and by the action of certain quick-acting chemicals which encourage the formation of 'hardpan.' The friability of the soil is reduced and runoff of water is increased accompanied by erosion and loss of nutrients.*

*Third, many commercial fertilizers are inimical to soil life, including earthworms.*

*Fourth, overbalance of certain chemicals prevents plants from absorbing some needed nutrients, thus altering the protein and vitamin contents of certain crops. Inorganic fertilizers are lacking in trace elements. Some fungus and bacterial diseases of plants have been related to high nitrogen fertilization and lack of trace elements.*

*The numbers on fertilizer bags (4-12-4 or 5-10-5) stand for nitrogen, phosphorous, and potassium percentages, or NPK percentage. The percentages above are those recommended for general use in commercial fertilizers. Organic fertilizers are long lasting and slow acting and economically used by the plant, with less leaching from soil. The percentages of basic nutrients need not be as high (percentages run about 2-5-2 on the average) as those in chemical fertilizers.*

*Compost is soil's natural balancing agent,*
*building up and breaking down.*
*Through its chemistry*
*"It grows such sweet things out of such corruptions . . .*
*It gives such divine materials to man, and accepts such leavings*
*from them at last."\**

*\*Walt Whitman."This Compost,"*
*Leaves of Grass.*

73 74 75   12 11 10 9 8 7 6 5 4 3 2 1